CAPTAIN WHISKERS

CAPTAIN WHISKERS

JEREMY STRONG

Illustrated by
Matt Robertson

Barrington Stoke

First published in 2020 in Great Britain by
Barrington Stoke Ltd
18 Walker Street, Edinburgh, EH3 7LP

www.barringtonstoke.co.uk

A CIP catalogue record for this book is available
from the British Library upon request

ISBN: 978-1-78112-927-2

Printed in China by Leo

This book is in a super-readable format for young readers
beginning their independent reading journey.

For Santi and family,
with added purring – JS

To Minnie – MR

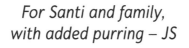

CONTENTS

CHAPTER 1

Pets

Hattie had a dog. Luke had a rabbit. Mahad had a lizard. Everyone in Jackson's class had a pet. Everyone except Jackson. Even Jackson's teacher, Miss Raza, had a pet. It was a parrot. Sometimes the parrot came to school with Miss Raza. It was called Billy Boy and it sat on a perch in one corner.

Sometimes Billy Boy shouted at the children: "Stop talking!" He sounded like their teacher and it made the children laugh. Miss Raza would blush and tell Billy Boy to stop being a pest. Sometimes the parrot spoke back: "Don't be a pest!" Then the children fell off their chairs laughing.

Miss Raza didn't bring her parrot to school very often.

Jackson thought everyone had a pet apart from him. He wanted one. Of course he did have his little brother but Freddie wasn't exactly a pet. Humans are animals of course, and pets are animals too, but you can't throw sticks for your brother or sister to fetch, can you?

On the other hand you don't have to clean up the mess they make.

Yuk! That idea made Jackson feel sick. Clean up his little brother? Freddie was only two and still had nappies.

But Jackson did want a pet. He liked the idea of looking after a dog or a cat. Something he could stroke and talk to. Something warm and friendly. Something that didn't answer back and tell him to "go away" or "pick up your clothes".

He asked his parents, "Can we have a dog?"

"They bark at night and wake everyone up," said Mum.

Dad grunted. "I sleep badly already. A dog would wake me up."

Mum nodded. "You know how grumpy your father can be in the morning."

It was true. Jackson's father simply could not sleep properly. It made him a bit grumpy. He didn't want to be grumpy but that is what happens if you don't get enough sleep.

"All right, how about a cat?" Jackson asked.

"They leave their hair everywhere and their bottoms look like pencil sharpeners," said Mum. She wasn't being very helpful.

Jackson sighed. "A hamster or a guinea pig?"

Dad shook his head. "I don't like ratty things. I had a friend who kept pet rats and one of them bit me."

Dad held up his finger and looked at it sadly as if it still hurt.

Mum laughed. "You told me you were nine when that happened. It was thirty years ago!"

"Maybe," Dad said. "But I don't want it to happen again."

"All right," sighed Jackson. "How about a stick insect?"

"Too sticky!" said Dad, and he laughed at his own joke.

Jackson didn't think it was funny.

He just wanted a friendly pet. He wasn't very good at making friends or chatting.

Most days he stood on his own in the playground and watched the others run around laughing and shouting.

He wanted to join in and be part of it but he was too shy to ask. What if the others said "No!"?

So he didn't dare ask.

CHAPTER 2

The Man With The Top Hat

One morning Jackson was on his way to school.

He was walking along thinking about other things when suddenly he heard loud barking.

A big black and white cat sped round the corner. It ran up to Jackson and straight up onto his head with all its fur standing on end.

A large dog raced round the corner after the cat. It had sharp teeth, a nasty growl and a wicked gleam in its eyes.

Jackson didn't run away. He stood very still and shouted at the dog: "GO!"

The dog slid to a stop, looked at Jackson, then turned round and trotted off with its tail between its legs.

Jackson invited the cat down from his head. He stroked it softly until it had calmed down and started to purr.

"Oh! You've rescued Mrs Wilson for me! How very kind."

Jackson looked up from the cat and saw an odd-looking man standing in front of him.

The man was tall and seemed even taller because he was wearing a top hat. He also had a huge smile on his face.

Jackson had never seen anyone actually wearing a top hat. It was silvery-grey and had a blue band around the rim. The man had a long grey beard and thin silver-rimmed glasses. A red spotted handkerchief was sticking out of the top pocket of his jacket. He was wearing shoes made of black and white leather and he had a walking stick with a round silver top.

Now the man bent down and patted Mrs Wilson on the head.

"Well, aren't you a lucky cat?" said The Man With The Top Hat.

Mrs Wilson purred even more loudly and settled into Jackson's arms. Then she turned onto her back, showing her furry white tummy for Jackson to stroke.

The Man With The Top Hat was impressed. "Well, well, Jackson," he said. "Mrs Wilson doesn't normally behave like that or purr as loud as that."

"How do you know my name?" asked Jackson.

"You told me," said The Man With The Top Hat.

"No, I didn't," Jackson insisted.

The Man With The Top Hat shook his head. "Well, there's a mystery then."

"Anyhow," Jackson went on, "Mrs Wilson is a very good name for a cat."

"She's a very good cat," answered The Man With The Top Hat. "And she chose that name. She told me so herself."

Jackson laughed. "Cats can't talk," he said.

The Man With The Top Hat gave a little smile. "Oh, I think you'll find they can. They just speak very softly, except to each other of course. Then they sometimes shout."

Mrs Wilson began to lick Jackson's hand and nibble one of his fingers.

"Mrs Wilson thinks my finger is a sausage," he said.

"You have a natural way with animals," said The Man With The Top Hat. "I expect you have lots of pets."

Jackson shook his head. He didn't say anything.

"Oh. Such a shame. I've got too many. You could have some of mine."

"That would be good," laughed Jackson. He put Mrs Wilson back on the ground. "I'd better get to school or I'll be late. Bye."

As Jackson set off, The Man With The Top Hat cried after him. "I have plenty of cats. I'll send you some of mine!"

"Great! How many?" Jackson shouted back.

"Will a hundred be OK?" asked the man.

Jackson laughed. He thought that The Man With The Top Hat was joking.

But he wasn't.

CHAPTER 3

Different Sorts of Surprises

Surprises are odd things. Some can be wonderful. Some can be scary. Some can be enormous and some can be very, very small.

When Jackson got home from school in the afternoon he found a surprise. It was both wonderful *and* a bit scary.

The first thing Jackson saw was his parents. They were sitting on the roof of the house. Mum had Jackson's little brother, Freddie, on her lap. Dad was throwing bits of roof tiles into the garden.

This was because the garden was full of cats.

There were cats everywhere. They weren't just in the garden, either. There were cats in the bedrooms and cats in the bath. There were cats in the cupboards and cats in the saucepans.

Jackson tried to count how many there were. He didn't really need to. In his heart he knew that there were a hundred. A hundred cats in his house. Mum and Dad were not very happy.

"They're eating the furniture!" cried Mum. (They weren't.)

"They've messed in my sock drawer!" Dad moaned. (They hadn't.)

Dad picked up another broken tile from the roof and threw it at the cats in the garden.

Maybe as the tile whizzed past one cat's head, the cat HISSED. But Jackson was absolutely sure that the cat said "MISSED!" – and then laughed. Ha ha ha!

There was another weird thing. Jackson knew the cat's name. He was called Captain Whiskers.

Somehow Jackson knew ALL the cats' names.

There was Jimbo, Bumble, Spottybot and Moonbeam.

There was Crumble, Milady, Trot and How-do-you-do.

There was Mr Banana, Flathead, Hooligan and Dinosaur Derek.

There was Floozy, Florence, Fat Fred and, of course, Captain Whiskers.

That was just 16 of them. There were
85 more, all of them with names. If you
are good at maths you will know that
85 and 16 makes 101 cats altogether.
Maybe The Man With The Top Hat was
not good at counting. Maybe he was.
We shall see.

All in all there were an awful lot
of cats around the place and an angry
mother and father sitting on the roof
with a Freddie that needed a new nappy.

Dad rang the police but all he got
was a recording.

"*We are out. There's a major criminal at large. Someone stole the Chief Constable's packed lunch and we are all hunting for the thief.*"

Dad rang the Fire Brigade.

"Are any of the cats on fire?" the Fire Brigade asked. "No? Sorry, we can't help you."

Mum and Dad looked down at
Jackson. What was he going to do?

CHAPTER 4

What the Cats Sang

Jackson's parents thought the cats were Jackson's fault. In a way they were right, but they were also wrong. Jackson had never asked for a hundred cats. Even so, everyone could see how much the cats liked Jackson.

They purred at him in a giant cat song. They rubbed up against him and curled their long tails round his legs. They sat on his lap and in his arms. Captain Whiskers sat on his head.

And of course Jackson spoke to the cats. Jackson was surprised that they listened to him.

"I like all of you," he told the cats. "But this house belongs to my family and we don't have room for you."

"Plenty of room," sang the cats in a way that was not helpful.

"No, there isn't," Jackson insisted.

"Mmmm. Yes," the cats argued. "We're staying. Good night." And they all curled up where they were and went to sleep. The sound of heavy purring rose into the air.

"This is ridiculous," snapped Dad as he came down from the roof. "I'm going to make supper and if any of these cats think they are getting some they can think again."

Jackson saw that Captain Whiskers opened one eye. Or was the cat winking at him?

*

The cats stayed in the house all night. In fact, Captain Whiskers curled up right next to Dad, who never even noticed.

Dad and Captain Whiskers both slept deeply and without dreams all night. When Dad opened his eyes he found he was nose to nose with Captain Whiskers. The cat was staring at him.

"OUT!" yelled Dad. But somehow he didn't sound grumpy. (That was because he had a laugh deep inside him. The laughter was so deep inside that Dad didn't know it was there, but it was.)

*

That morning the cats went to school
with Jackson. They crowded into Miss
Raza's classroom. Billy Boy had come to
school with Miss Raza that day. He was
cross and upset about having the cats in
the classroom.

"Police! Fire! Earthquake!" squawked
Billy Boy.

Captain Whiskers put a paw on Billy Boy's perch and looked hard at the parrot.

"Don't be a pest," said Captain Whiskers.

Billy Boy was so surprised that the cat had stolen his words that he said nothing else for the rest of the day.

The children thought it was wonderful to have so many cats in school. The cats went everywhere.

They jumped on the computer in the office so that the secretary typed all the wrong words in the letter she was writing to parents.

During Assembly the cats walked across Miss Raza's piano when the children were singing.

PING! PANG! PONG! "OW!" That was Miss Raza shouting. Two cats had just shut the piano lid on her hands.

By the end of the day everyone was talking to Jackson, the boy with a hundred cats. In fact now he had a hundred friends. But the teachers were pleased to see all the cats follow Jackson home. Billy Boy was pleased too.

CHAPTER 5

The Man With The
Top Hat Has a Secret

By this time even Jackson knew that a
hundred cats was too many. He had
only wanted one pet. He couldn't keep
a hundred cats at home or have them at
school every day.

"You really must go," he told the cats. "I never asked for so many. I thought The Man With The Top Hat was joking."

"He wasn't," said Captain Whiskers. "Anyway, there aren't a hundred of us. There are a hundred and one. I am the extra one. I am staying because you can only send a hundred cats back and, anyway, I am YOUR cat."

"Mum and Dad won't let me have a cat," Jackson told him. "They don't like pets."

Captain Whiskers gave a sigh. "They just need to get used to the idea. They will soon fall in love with me. You wait and see. The other cats will go back."

The other cats left. Jackson's parents hunted high and low to make sure that they had all gone.

They soon found Captain Whiskers. He was lying across the sofa watching television.

"Out you go!" said Mum.

Captain Whiskers jumped down. He curled his tail round their legs. He purred hard. He sat down at their feet and stared up at them with the biggest, wettest, most charming eyes EVER.

Dad looked into the very same eyes he had seen so close up that morning. He remembered how well he had slept and how good he felt when he got up. He hadn't been grumpy all day.

Mum looked at Dad. Dad looked at Mum. Freddie looked at Captain Whiskers.

"Want!" said Freddie.

Jackson held his breath.

"WANT!" said Freddie, even more loudly.

Captain Whiskers rolled over and showed everyone his soft, white, furry tummy.

"I suppose," began Mum. "I suppose we might ..."

"Just for a day or two," added Dad. "Let's see."

And that was when Jackson knew that Captain Whiskers really was his cat and was going to stay with him always.

*

Jackson didn't have a hundred cats. But often the other cats came to visit and have a chat with Captain Whiskers and Jackson.

There was Six Toe Sam, Dora Dash and Jim-Jam-Joe. There was Squiffy, Whiffy and Uncle Baggy-Pants. There was Fancy-That, Cheesecake Charlie and Lord High-and-Mighty. There was Waddle, Puddle, Piddle and Pooh. And then there were all the others.

Sometimes Captain Whiskers would wait for Jackson outside school in the afternoon.

They would walk home together, and one day they met The Man With The Top Hat.

Captain Whiskers and Mrs Wilson were very happy to see each other, and so were Jackson and The Man With The Top Hat.

"Thank you," said Jackson.

"I didn't do anything," said The Man With The Top Hat.

"You sent a hundred and one cats to my house," said Jackson.

"Oh? I thought it was a hundred." The Man With The Top Hat winked. "I'm so happy you're looking after Captain Whiskers."

"Actually, I think he's looking after me," said Jackson. "We're good at chatting."

"I'm so pleased to hear that," said The Man With The Top Hat. "Be good and take care. Goodbye."

*

After that an odd thing happened. Jackson began to think that talking to cats was easy.

Then he began to think that talking to the children at school was easy too.

All he had to do was pretend that everyone at school was a cat. Even Miss Raza and the other teachers.

But what Jackson never knew was that The Man With The Top Hat had a secret.

Underneath the top hat was another, rather different, kind of hat.

Our books are tested
for children and young people by
children and young people.

Thanks to everyone who consulted on
a manuscript for their time and effort in
helping us to make our books better
for our readers.